Kisses on the Wind

Kisses on the Wind

Lisa Moser

illustrated by Kathryn Brown

CANDLEWICK PRESS

ON THE DAY we left for Oregon, I said good-bye
to the barn cats. I said good-bye to the farmhouse.
But I just couldn't say good-bye to Grandma.

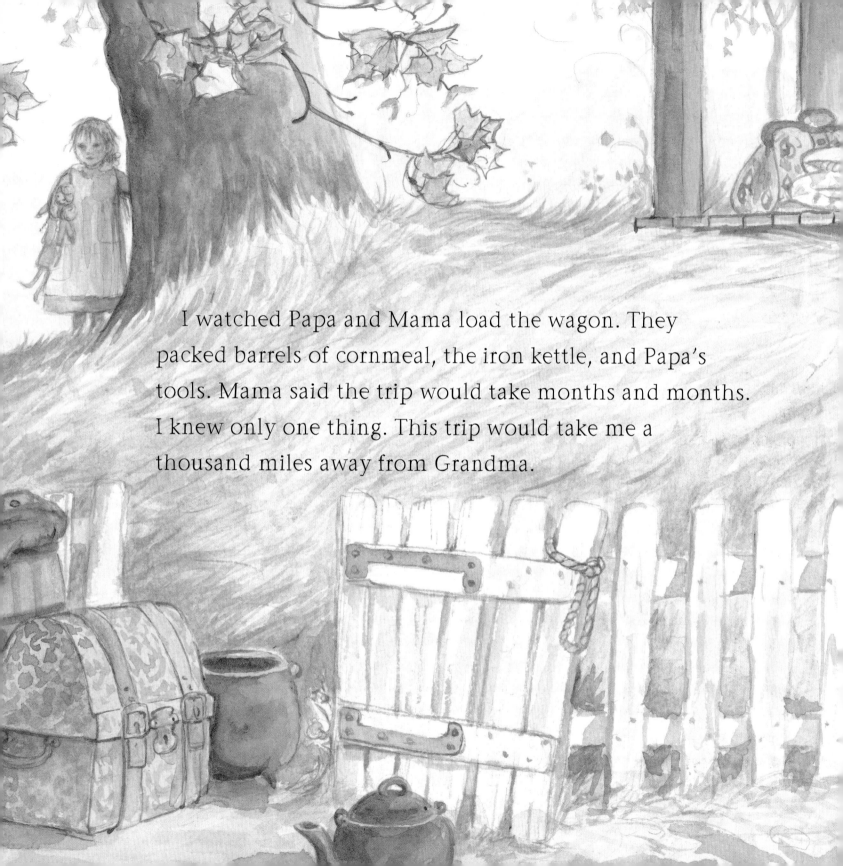

I watched Papa and Mama load the wagon. They packed barrels of cornmeal, the iron kettle, and Papa's tools. Mama said the trip would take months and months. I knew only one thing. This trip would take me a thousand miles away from Grandma.

I ran to the barn and hid. I figured if they
couldn't find me, they couldn't make me go.
Just when I was about to burst with sadness,
I peeked between the cracks.

Grandma was sitting on the swing.

I ran out. "What are you doing, Grandma?"

"Lydia, darling! I was just picturing," said Grandma.

"Picturing what?" I asked.

"You swinging to the treetops. Me pushing and telling stories." She sighed and stood up. "I'm going to do a lot of picturing. It will help me with the missing."

I kicked at the dirt. "I don't want to go," I said.

"I know," said Grandma. She reached for my hand. We started walking.

Grandma and I walked through the woods.
We hunted for wildflowers and leaves and pieces
of bark, just the right size. Then we made a bark
boat together.

"We've been making bark boats since you were
just a mite bigger than the milking stool," said
Grandma.

I put my head in Grandma's lap and cried
a little. She held and rocked me. "That's right.
You let those tears come," she said.

When I was all cried out, we went to the pond.
Grandma pushed our bark boat into the water.
It sailed away. "When you miss me," said Grandma,
"teach a new friend how to make a bark boat."

For the longest time, I couldn't talk.
Finally, I said, "I will."

A robin flew by, and I jumped up. I wanted to run. I wanted to run all of the sadness out of my legs. I followed that robin, and Grandma followed me. We ran and laughed. It felt good. Then we rested in the tall, sweet grass.

Grandma sat close and braided my hair. Always gentle. *Weave. Weave. Tug. Weave. Weave. Tug.*

"When I was a little girl . . ." said Grandma, and then she was off on one of her stories. Grandma was full up of stories. Bedtime stories. Dish-washing stories. Butter-churning stories. And I loved every one.

I closed my eyes and listened until she finished. Then I asked, "Does picturing really help?"

"It helps me," said Grandma.

"This is how I will picture you. Braiding my hair, telling me a story. Like you do every morning."

Suddenly a terrible thought hit me. "Grandma," I said, "I can't go to Oregon. I'll miss the stories you tell."

Grandma reached into her apron pocket. She pulled out a brown book and laid it in my hands. "I wrote my stories down for you, Lydia. When you miss me, you can read them."

I opened the book that Grandma had made and turned the pages. Words floated by. Grandma's words. Grandma's stories. Stories she'd told since I was a baby.

I rubbed the smooth leather cover with my
hands. "Now you'll always be with me," I said.
"And every day I will think of you and love you."
"And I'll be loving you," said Grandma.

On our way back, Grandma and I climbed my favorite hill. I looked out over the farm and fields.

Then I hugged Grandma a long time. I breathed her in deep so I would not forget. I listened to her heartbeat and made my ears remember.

When I let go, I saw Papa hitching up the oxen.
I saw Mama folding my quilt. My family was ready
to leave. And I was, too.

"I have to go," I said.

"I know," said Grandma. I reached for her hand.
We started walking.

Grandma helped me tuck my doll into the wagon.

"When I miss you, I'll say a prayer for you," I said.

"I'll pray for all of you," said Grandma. "That's my best comfort."

Then we were hugging. Grandma, Mama, Papa, and me. One big mess of arms and hearts.

I climbed onto the wagon seat. Mama held my hand. Papa called to the oxen. The wagon creaked and rolled out of the farmyard.

I looked back.

Grandma stood at the gate. She touched her hands
to her lips. Then she flung her arms open wide.

I knew what she was doing. She was sending me
kisses on the wind.

I sent them right back to her.

In memory of my beloved grandma Helen I. Crockett.
She loved me so well, and I loved her right back.
L. M.

In memory of Grandma Ocie Brown,
and for Frankie, Summer, Sadie, & Brandi
K. B.

Text copyright © 2009 by Lisa Moser
Illustrations copyright © 2009 by Kathryn Brown

First edition 2009

Library of Congress Cataloging-in-Publication Data
Moser, Lisa.
Kisses on the wind / Lisa Moser ; illustrated by Kathryn Brown. —1st ed.
p. cm.
Summary: Young Lydia struggles to say goodbye to her grandmother as her parents finish packing their
wagon for the long journey to Oregon in the nineteenth century.
ISBN 978-0-7636-3110-9
[1. Moving, Household—Fiction. 2. Grandmothers—Fiction. 3. Frontier and pioneer life—Fiction.
4. West (U.S.)—History—To 1848—Fiction.] I. Brown, Kathryn, ill. II. Title.
PZ7.M84696Kis 2009
[E]—dc22   2008053490

2 4 6 8 10 9 7 5 3 1

Printed in China

This book was typeset in Godlike Emboldened.
The illustrations were done in watercolor.

Candlewick Press
99 Dover Street
Somerville, Massachusetts 02144

visit us at www.candlewick.com